Guardians Of

CW00400318

The Outersphere Warlord Monologues

Forward

After many long nights (gaming), I decided to write this, the second book in the Outersphere Warlord series after mishearing a quote on the radio. What follows is an even more convoluted and poorly thought out homage to all my friends and family… plus it didn't feel right leaving the book off where it was, as I had so much more material to work with.

I would also like to thank the *mysterious, wonderful, beautiful and glowing women I spend not enough time around* for without whom certain characters in this book wouldn't be possible, thanks for all the teas.

The Outersphere Warlord Monologues

5000 Degrees

"If you're going to fight, fight for honour, fight for justice, fight for those too weak to fight for themselves, fight for what is right, fight for everyone who stands behind and with you... unless you fight for money, then fight dirty"

This is what my mother always told me when I came home. She was the only person I ever knew who was proud of me for anything I did. Literally it didn't matter if I came back and told her I had just murdered an entire planet load of marines while they slept, she would always see the bright side... on that particular occasion she congratulated me and told me how proud she was that her son had "*such good tactical smarts like your dad*".

She even congratulated me for going into the Peacekeepers... Although, she couldn't actually come up with a good reason for it at the time... Actually she kind of fluffed over the fact that I was with them to be honest... She did make a big deal about how nice the uniform was, but a much bigger deal about the big box of doughnuts I brought back. She was always proud of me, no matter what I did, especially if I brought doughnuts.

I remember coming home after picking a fight with the school bully because he had beaten one of the smaller kids to a bloody pulp, he kicked my arse from one end of the settlement to the other, right up to the point that we reached the port… and then he pushed me into the harbour. I swam there, covered in seaweed, shit and refuse, as planned all along… I was a cunning little bastard even then. I started throwing shit at him till he jumped in to beat me some more, as soon as he did, I had won… he couldn't swim but was too stupid to remember. I got my first taste of blood that day, I beat him as he desperately tried to get out, and kept beating him till he finally sank below the surface. I will never forget the look of utter defeat on his face as he hung in my grasp as I dragged him back to shore. My mother never said anything about the smell or the blood stains, all she would say, was that she was so proud of her *"Hero Son what saved that poor kids life"*. That was the first time Benny really looked up to me as well. He was the young kid that got bullied that day. He never really fully recovered from the beating, as I may have told you before, he's about as intelligent as he is small… that is, he's huge, hulking, and dumber than two bald men fighting over a comb while sitting on a nuke falling through the clouds towards its intended target.

He grew up fast though Benny, he spent less and less time at school and more and more time at the local Gyms, docks, or anywhere he could get a job lifting heavy objects, or punching things. To the point that he got dropped from 4th grade for failing to spell 'Them' thirteen times in a row... although the hospitalising of the teacher who called him stupid may have also had something to do with it. At that time, he was pushing weights that made the professional lifters at the gym cringe and cower just at the thought of. He grew UP fast too, he was 6 feet by the time he was 8 years old, and 7 feet by the time his balls dropped. He quickly became my heavy muscle when fights broke out, and I quickly became his brains whenever he needed me to solve a complex problem... like why he couldn't get his door open, after spending three hours pushing on it, and I simply showed him that it just needed to be pulled... he still asks me to help him with that particular little brain teaser.

He didn't initially join the Phalanx with me, as he was representing the local gym at the time in a weight lifting competition... Or I should say, lifting the competition over his head before storming off with several of the female competitors, under his arms... he was under a lot of stress truth be told, that and suffering from raging hormones... probably induced by the small pharmacy he had eaten the day before.

Anyway, why do I bring this up? Well, it's because my mother dearest called a few days back and asked for us to come and help out, as:

"Some Centre douches were cracking down on the locals and causing a right ruckus, and its interfering with our poker night"

So, after Viola fixed the shields and got the main gun working again after the '300 faces of death' incident, which we survived by the way, only just but we did. We set off home.

I hadn't been home since before I left the peacekeepers, mainly as I wasn't allowed within thirty parsecs of the planet, but since I'm technically in charge of Outersphere now, I may as well drop some of the charges against me… I mean if you can't drop charges against yourself and your friends when you become the leader of a disparate and broken coalition of desperate and broken people, what's the point am I right?

Anyway, after kicking one of the Centre princes royal asses out of the area, along with 20,000 of the Centre's finest, we had them on the run, and everything was fine… right up to the point that the engines blew and started us plummeting towards the atmosphere at speeds that make ships such as ours turn into candles in furnaces… that is all melty like.

So, where was I? Oh yes, I had joined the phalanx and survived the initiation, then I told you about the promotion opportunity, but I never told you about the time we invaded the White Petal Corps then home, the reason this comes to mind, was that it was a similar situation, in that we were about to die a hot and melty death.

You see someone in the White Petal Corps had the bright idea to develop a new heat round that could burn through anything that it touched, and the Order wanted it for themselves. Those of you with good memories, and deep enough wallets and questionable intellect to have bought this books prequel, will remember I use something similar to this in my current guns... same tech, in fact, this was the prototype.

So there we were, all sitting in our Phalanx drop ships, when the word came down that we would be accompanied by the Valkyrie fleet from the Western Alliance. The Valkyries were galactic bigwigs with a reputation of getting shit done that almost equalled the OZ. The first of the girls aboard our drop ship was Cali... yes that Cali, this is how I met her, and no, we don't hook it up just yet, remember, I was still all puffed up about being a Phalanx, so I wasn't looking to sow seeds at this point in my life... plus I was still terrified to talk to girls... I know, hard to believe that I ever had any trouble speaking to women, but there you have it, we all come from somewhere.

Anyway, me and Benny were in the same squad by this point, and Cali was drafted into our squad as a liaison... a fancy term for *"person used to keep our squad from fucking things up too much"*. She was just as dangerous then as she is now, only probably more responsible... we soon changed that.

We were thundering our way across White Petal Corp space in our stealth drop ships, all ready to drop out of stealth and plummet to the planet's surface and then kill anything and everything in our path to the research facility, when Cali suggested that maybe we would be better suited to a tactical insertion just the four of us... in case you were wondering the fourth was Derv, but he's such a dull person to talk about, I will talk about him as little as possible... mainly because he never said ANYTHING of note the whole time we were there... though he certainly saved our asses on more than one occasion.

Anyway, after some 'discussion' which ended in a stalemate… and both me and Cali having black eyes and me having bruised shins, we decided that it would be better for inter-organisational diplomacy that we should do things Cali's way… basically she blabbed to the higher-ups that we were being mean.

So, we got put in this small tight drop shit of a ship, and plopped at the far side of the planet to where we needed to be… why we were dropped so far from the intended target is still beyond me, but it ended up being a good thing, as it gave us far more time to get used to how White Petal folks actually did things… I think I may have told you about their naming conventions for things, well, I'm going to again... they take an inordinate amount of time to actually say much at all, so most of them spend days on end never talking about anything, or weeks just ordering breakfast.

We were dropped off outside of a religious conclave full of nuns, and had I been like I am today, that would have been a story in and of itself, but as it was, we actually avoided it… probably a good thing too, I am pretty sure I would be old and grey before I managed to actually woo one of those nuns what with describing my many talents in a white petal manner…

Plus, these weren't the naughty sexy kind of nuns that had tight fitting habits that were cropped at the knee, and looked like the goddess Freya had been cloned and the clones had all taken up residence in a nunnery all awaiting their heroic and sexy Warlord to come and whisk them away from their lives of celibacy to a world of dirty and erotic bed time naughtiness all by an open fire…

No instead these were the kind of nuns that make priests behave themselves… and school children fear them for the rest of their lives… you know, the ones that if you picked one up and swung it at a tree, the tree would get up and run away.

Anyway, we started to make our way into a nearby forest to lose the tracking unit that had been dispatched to our location once our drop shit of a ship lit up on all of their long range scanners as it gracefully and gently crashed head first into a swamp… I suppose looking back on it, that may have been a good thing, as the white petal corp trackers were convinced that it was just a meteor that they called off the search after a week… this may sound like a long time, but that's just how long it took them to say "*It's not here, don't know what happened to it boss*"… or that is what I imagine they were trying to do all that time anyway. So there we were, on a strange planet, full of people who were all trained killers, and all took thirteen minutes in the morning to say "*Hello*". Cali set about immediately dictating what we should and shouldn't do, and I immediately set about ignoring her, and doing things my own way… Yes her approach was probably the more controlled and appropriate, but hers would have also taken months to complete. It's amazing how much she has changed over the years thinking back on it… she used to be so controlled and strict…

Now she just blows shit up for the fun of it…

Strange what life does to people.

Anyway, my plan was simple, we would hitchhike to the nearest airfield and steal a "*Swims-among-the-stars-like-a-shining-swallow-tailed-flying-fish*" or light aircraft as I call it. Then fly the thing to the city next to the research station, then spend a few days having R and R, right before actually storming the research station, and then making a mad rush for the hidden jump ship that was carefully being readied by Order operatives as we spoke, it was a sound plan… except for one small oversight… The white petal corps had not only discovered the Order Operatives a few hours after we landed, but had also banned all flights on or around research facility planets during the final stages of research.

When we got to the nearest airfield, there wasn't a single plane taking off or flying… this made the stealthy option of flying in under radar a little academic, as anyone with a set of eyes would see us coming from a mile away… although thinking back on it, they wouldn't have been able to describe what they saw quick enough for us to be in any danger.

So we stole an"*Armoured-Like-A-Preying-Mantis-Perched-Upon-The-Back-Of-A-Giant-Turtle-And-Ready-To-Strike-At-Its...*" you know what, it was an Armoured Personnel Carrier, I'm not going to give you the full name as I don't have the patience, memory, nor spare space on my storage disc for the name. Sufficed to say that the acronym is fifty two letters long, and even that is too bloody long to say, so APC will have to do.

Anyway, we stole the surprisingly comfortable APC and started making our way cross country and under the radar. This was where Cali started to get the jitters for things that go Boom. You see we had stolen an APC with a heavy grenade launcher attached to the top, and since Cali was the only one who was small enough to fit into the seat... and because it was a separate cabin, and we were more than a little annoyed at her incessant complaints of "*intergalactic treaty*" this and "*war-crime*" that, she got to sit in the gunner seat.

It all went sideways when we were approaching a local town looking to get some fuel for the gas guzzling, but incredibly comfortable, APC, when I shouted back to Cali to wake up and keep her head on swivel. This caused her to jump a little and accidentally let off a shot from the grenade launcher. This would have been fine, except we were passing an oil refinery at the time, that was unfortunately next to an ammo dump, a fireworks factory, and several fuel storage depots too… Things got a little heated at that point. The fireball could be seen for one hundred miles in either direction, and actually caused damage to several satellites that were orbiting just above the epicentre.

It was at this point, that all idea of stealth would normally have gone to shit, but apparently, the police investigating the fire spent so long calling it in, and getting more fire fighters on scene, that the whole place was a crispy black smouldering hole, and no evidence could be found as to what caused it. This would normally have been considered a serious turn of good luck for us, but Cali had tasted the forbidden fruit, and nothing anyone said could convince her to change her mind... plus none of us could get a word in edgeways what with her constant laughing and giggle fits. Anyway, she seemed to be having fun so we left her to it... plus none of us could actually get her out of the gunners cabin as it was too small for any of us to actually get a hold of her.

The news services were the first to notice the pattern that was being drawn across the landscape with explosions and fires randomly starting up and taking over entire towns, they noted how they all seemed to originate by the site of the first 'accident' and travelled at an approximate speed of fifty miles an hour (the top speed of the APC), and that maybe people should evacuate along the route as there was clearly a gas main that was running along there that was connected to the original explosion. This prompted the research facility to be abandoned by the time we got to it, which was handy… and Cali claims to this date was her plan all along… which I doubt as all you could hear from in the back was various forms of the following

"*Boom!*"

"*Die Bitches!*"

"*Why won't you fucking die… oh, you already did*"

And my favourite

"*What do you mean I'm out of Ammo! It's an Energy based Grenade Launcher… as long as we have gas I have Boom Time!*" followed by "*Ooh silly me, the launcher overheated… I can fix that…*"

This was followed by a pit stop at a local hardware store where Cali showed us one of her other many talents, that is 'cobbling shit together to make for more explosions'... she also found that you could take the safety off of the launcher so that it didn't stop firing when it overheated... but that if you carried on, the barrel would melt, so she changed the barrel for a more heat resistant version... so on and so on. To be honest, she kind of came up with some serious improvements to the design of the launcher, it was just a 'shame' that she left it planet side when we had to get out, those design changes have been implemented across the board with all military grenade launchers now, and everyone keeps claiming they did it first, when in fact it was little Cali... she could have been a multi-billionaire by now with the copyright... well she couldn't... She would still have been shooting things with the Grenade Launcher today if we hadn't 'accidentally' had to steal a ship that was too small to fit the APC in... She is still sore about that. Still, it brought us all a bit of cheer in a boring adventure. To be honest, she really gelled us together as a group as well, don't tell her, but she is actually one of the reasons I wanted to start our own mercenary group in the first place.

We never really got much of a chance to work with the Valkyries after that incident, especially since she defected and joined the Phalanx about a week later... said she had differences of opinion with her superiors about the use of lethal force on the firing range... the bunkhouse... the dining hall... and during her disciplinary hearings. Basically, she was perfect for the Phalanx at the time... and quickly became one of our most valued squad mates... even if we never got invited to stealth missions ever again.

Oh, there was a point when leaving the planet that we were surrounded, and if it hadn't been for Derv's first shot hitting the first thirteen guys between the eyes, we may have had a problem. But it doesn't seem that impressive looking back, that's why I almost forgot about it... that and I hate mentioning Derv at all, you can almost feel the fun being sucked out of the atmosphere when he starts talking... Don't get me wrong, I wouldn't want anyone else watching my back... but I certainly wouldn't want to be in earshot of him...

or sight of him…

or have him in the same room as me…

Come to think of it, it's only the fact that he is an ungodly shot that we haven't shot him yet. You know, he once managed to close an all-night Burlesque show… just by asking for a drink at the bar… I have never seen so many people lose interest in tits and ass quicker in my entire life… and I once saw Benny naked…

Look, it's not that he is depressed, or that he looks bad… far from it, he has his own line of very popular hair products named after him back in the centre after all… No, it's just that he is SO bloody boring… I mean watching paint dry… in slow motion… while its underwater… without lights… and listening to 23rd century pop kind of boring… you know, enough to make you want to pull the airlocks open and suffocate yourself to death kind of boring… he has such a vacuous personality that I swear I even lost interest in finishing what I was going to say… I just… AAarrgh!

Anyway, that melty death I was telling you was going to thankfully happen shortly reminded me of the time the Phalanx had a beach getaway... I say beach getaway, we attacked a planet that was literally nothing but endless blue sea and beaches, and people like Derv surfing and letting their hair look like some kind of weird commercial for Derv Haircare Products... *"One Shot Is All You Need"*... Sorry about that, he roped me into a commercial once, and I get a percentage of the proceeds consequently... One of the generals wanted to have a seaside residence, and someone told him that the Eastern Eagle Cooperative had a planet that had the perfect spot for one... so the whole of the Phalanx was mobilised and sent to invade this little backwater of a planet and claim it for the Order. It was just a shame that it also happened to be the EEC's officer getaway weekend when we arrived. We ended up turning half of the planet to glass, and the other half into a still smoking crater... well not all of the planet was ruined, the generals house was finished on the only part that was still ok. He still lives there actually, he doesn't mind the smell of Sulphur in the morning, tells everyone it

"*Smells like Victory*"… I think it smells more like one of Benny's socks myself… but it made him happy, and we all got a serious pay raise after wiping out the EEC's entire upper echelons in one day. It probably didn't help them that they all came without weapons, but hey, a victory is a victory right?

It was on this barbeque on the beach that we met Sally actually come to think of it…

She was the head of one of the other Phalanx squads from out east and was well versed in Anti EEC tactics… That is she had an awful lot of bounties out on her for war-crimes against the EEC… Most of which entailed skinning people alive, and sending them back alive in body bags filled with salt… She had quite the reputation, and the reputation never quite lived up to her.

Anyway, she was drafted into our unit as most of her guys quit the week before after the last time she had gone on a rampage... I guess they thought we could temper her rage somewhat. Instead of that, what happened was they created one of the most deadly fighting units the Phalanx had ever seen. Our success rate is still the stuff of legends... and many pending war-crimes tribunals should any of us ever actually be captured... You know I said I could get most of the charges against me and the guys dropped... there are limits to power... but not peoples memory... or written record... or video footage apparently... or the fact that Sally may have used a few of the locals as her own personal etch-a-sketch...

It also turned out that she is a wiz behind the wheel. We were on some downtime on one of the Red Sunlight District Planets, you know... for the 'culture'... we were enjoying this great show by a nice girl who ended up being my 8th wife a few years later after a stint keeping my head down in her 'establishment'... anyway, Edie had just finished her show and was just collecting her tips with her buttocks while spinning upside down, when a bunch of Peacekeepers burst in to collect on the bounties of anyone who happened to be wanted at the time... well, we made sure Edie finished her set properly, and gave her a bonus for professionalism for managing to keep smiling even when one of the peacekeepers hands landed squarely on her tits... just his hand mind you... the rest of him was being torn to pieces by Sally and Cali for interrupting their session of 'Guess The Strippers Natural Hair Colour Before The Knickers Come Off'. Anyway, Edie finished her set, proceeded to wipe the guts from the feathers in her hair, then beat the shit out of the remaining 12 Peacekeepers who had been brought in for backup, while me and Benny finished our drinks... right before getting stuck into the three APCs that turned up after Edie made mincemeat of the poor bastard whose eye popped out and landed between her cleavage.

Anyway, things were going swimmingly, and we were having a ball of a time smashing heads together and listening to Edie sing as she and Sally broke three guys necks between their combined cleavage, when the sky went dark and the Peacekeeper Super-cruiser "*The Deft Hand*" turned up and started shouting all sorts of demands. Anyway, we jumped in the nearest vehicle and made a run for it, I mean I'm all for impossible odds, but 6 against 60,000 in mech suits just wasn't a win-win situation for anyone but the Peacekeepers... and no one likes a sore winner.

Sally was the first into the vehicle, but Derv said something about women drivers, and got a look that to this day makes even me want to hide and hope the storm will go away. Anyway, the others piled into the back, and Sally started the engine, and in a wall of tire smoke she took the fuck off like nothing I have ever seen. I swear she can make things go faster than they ought just by shear will power and ego alone.

Anyway, the 60,000 green mech suit wearing namby-pamby Peacekeepers, who later would be my esteemed colleagues, tried to surround us and stop us getting to our transport ship we had at the port... what followed was like something out of Transporter 315 Part Two, we went from screeching tires to screeching passengers, to screeching Peacekeepers as we must have made mach 5 or 6 on four wheels, while traveling sideways down a one way street... the wrong way... and she managed to get the damned thing through rush-hour traffic without so much as spilling the drink she still had in her hands... Derv has not once since questioned a woman's driving... so at least one of us grew that day... the rest of them lost at least six years of their lives in sheer terror... not at being captured, but at the prospect of being killed either by Sally's insane ability to make a 16 wheeler go round corners that are tight even when walking, or the fact that when anyone of them tried to get out and surrender, she threatened to drive back and start over again. I think I was the only one enjoying the ride, and totally didn't make out with her... twelve times... while she piloted the transport ship through a blockade of 42 Super-Cruisers and 60 or so cruisers at speeds that most ships use for interstellar travel, let alone leaving port… great times. Unlike today, where our engines are about as on fire as our outer hull, and even Sally has put two hands on to the controls… this is only the second time I have seen her do that in all the time I have known her.

The other time was during a Peacekeeping mission to the Northern Peoples Republic of D'hor, a series of five planets and suns orbiting a rouge black hole that was in its infancy.

We were sent in to sort out some internal power struggle that had led to thirteen billion refugees and a space jam that covered three systems. Apparently the Supreme Ultimate Leader had died and left two children in line for the throne, namely Princess Cira, and Princess Michelle. One was a moderate who wanted to bring the NPRD into the intergalactic fold, while the other was a crazy lunatic who wanted to push the galaxy into a conflict that would burn the light from every star system and leave only the NPRD left standing… or so she said.

We had been brought in to 'oversee' the rule of law, and ensure that the internal method of deciding the lines of succession didn't spill out of control and into a three system wide ethnic cleansing... it sounded much more magnanimous than it was, the Peacekeepers actually had a base on one of the systems moons... an expensive base... a 'newly-built-a-few-months-before' base... finished just two days before the Supreme Ultimate Leader had passed away tragically in an 'Accident' involving his space suit and the black hole that he apparently got too close too while in his bath... If you can work out why he was in a space suit in his bath, and why his bath was situated too close to a black hole... when it was planet side... you have done better than 99% of the people who live in the NPRD... who still think the galaxy is flat and revolves around them.

The Peacekeeper base had sent a distress call after the Princess Michelle had decided that she wanted a new base of operations and liked the colour scheme the Peacekeepers had chosen, and we were sent in.

This was one of the few occasions where Derv didn't go, as he was busy shooting a new Hair Commercial on the Jungle planet of Trope, and consequently, this is one of the few occasions where we had a damned fun time… despite the abject misery and filth that the locals lived in, nothing could possibly depress us about the situation as we didn't have Derv with us… I'm pretty sure if he had been there, we would have all committed suicide.

The general in charge of the Peacekeeper base, General Octavius (yes that was his name… and yes he was a pompous ass), called specifically for my unit as we had a reputation for getting shit done. He called us into his gold gilded office and had the four of us (Me, Sally, Cali and Benny) standing to attention while some waif of a boy fed him grapes like he was the emperor of the universe. He was old and about as fat as he was tall, making him look like some weird crossbreed between a football and raisin. He looked us over, smiled (revealing no teeth), and spluttered his orders to us. He said something like

"Don't kill too many locals. Don't make too many enemies. And most importantly don't work with the resistance at all"

So the first thing we did was make contact with the local resistance in order to get the skinny on what was going on where, and who was behind it all. The resistance sent their two most skilled operatives, one Darren and Sara O'Brian… yes, this is where we met the terrible twins.

I first laid eyes on my fifth wife when one of her battle bots was pinned on top of me with its chainsaw buzzing near my nose, she walked into the room like there was nothing going on and grabbed a wrench and started working on what to me looked like a pile of scrap metal, which later turned into an assault class Rider with Gatling Lasers and missile launcher. She took one look at me and fell head over heels in love with me… or at least that's what I like to think… she actually said *"Hurry up and kill it before it gets up"*, she was always such a kidder.

Anyway, after Darren came in and vouched for me, and I let the battle bot escape its certain demise, she started to take a shine to me... she hit me over the head with the wrench and warned me that "*If you have damaged the servos on Polly?! I will replace them with the ones keeping your leg working, you half tin, half tuna freak!*"

We hit it off like a house on fire after that.

The trouble started after we accidentally shot Princess Michelle when we went to try and 'Peacekeep' during a conference between the two siblings. This apparently set Princess Cira off, and set the stage for the first of the many Peacekeeper Wars. All I will say is that we had no intention of shooting her in the face, and we certainly weren't receiving a large pay packet from the resistance at the time....

Anyway, things were going really well at the conference right up to the point that the Princess Michelle demanded that the Peacekeepers disarm during the conference, and that outside interference would result in a "*Fire and Fury the likes of which the universe hasn't seen since the first big bang*", it was then that someone who looked a lot like me had a gun misfire and caused Princess Michelle to lose her left eye, and half of her head.

Princess Cira then went all biblical on us and tried to kill everyone in the room while her sister was rushed off to the nearest med bay. It's strange, the moderate sister ended up being just as crazy as the crazy sister… I guess blood really is thicker than water.

Anyway, Princess Michelle survived, and the two sisters became the best of friends and put all differences aside, so we had done what we had set out to do… unite the NPRD all under the banner of one crazy family, and start one of the most deadly conflicts in the history of the northern quadrants.

I still get hate mail even today.

I swear I just heard part of the outer hull pop off…
never mind….
So where was I, oh yes…

Darren and Sara didn't initially join the peacekeepers,
mainly as there was the issue of outstanding warrants
and war crime tribunals to take care of, but no
witnesses ever came forward, and all the charges
were dropped when one of the lead investigators
daughters disappeared for a few weeks right as
proceedings had started. Now I'm not suggesting that
Darren had anything to do with her disappearance,
and subsequent reappearance a few weeks later,
pregnant with his first child, but the two of them
became very close during the investigations. I am
also not saying that she had anything to do with the
strange illness that killed off only those people who
had actually witnessed Darren murdering a village
load of NPRD troops, but Celia did happen to be a top
virologist studying the weaponisation of certain
deadly viruses.

Darren and her got married a few weeks later, and we all went on a massive drinking binge that covered 300 different pubs over the space of 3 days. As I said at the time 'They were the best of times, they were the worst of times'… I read that somewhere once.

No, Darren and Sara didn't join the Peacekeepers at first, in fact we didn't see them again until a few years later when I was investigating a daring raid on a financial planet that had resulted in the loss of a lot of Centre resources. The gang I suspected of performing this heist somehow managed to get away, and we never did find out who the ring leader was… all we know was that he had a mechanical left arm, leg, and eye… he also had some short stock of a woman with him that kept throwing grenades and sticks of explosive around while singing… there was a tall goddess of a woman who was complaining about not being allowed to murder everything… and some tank of a guy who lifted the vault over his head and walked it to their waiting totally stolen Peacekeeper dropship. Funny coincidence, that years Peacekeeper ball was the most decadent and expensive affair the Peacekeepers had ever seen.

While I was investigating the possible links between the local taverns, I came across Darren and Sara involved in a shootout with the local authorities that made the old western classic John Wick Series look kind of tame. It wasn't until I convinced the local authorities that Darren and Sara were informants in my case, and that maybe they would survive to see another dawn, that they thought it was a good idea to let bygones be bygones, and surrender the workshop they were hid up in back to Darren and Sara.

I had to convince my higher ups that this was a good thing, and deputised Darren and Sara to avoid a conflict of interest.

It was shortly after this that they both got their nicknames, Violence and Violates.

It had come to our attention that some higher ups were questioning the statements that we had collected from the bank heist, and that there was a pirate group in the area that had gotten a name for itself for attacking and killing people… I mean what kind of pirate group goes around stealing and killing stuff… anyway, as a distraction… I mean target of opportunity, we decided that me, Darren and Sara would infiltrate the pirate gang, and arrest the whole lot of them once we got them all in one place.

Darren decided that the best way to get himself into the pirate gang, was to kill their main competition and bring their heads on a platter to the pirate leader, a fella by the name of Captain Hook… I'm not kidding, that was his actual name… first name Captain, last name Hook… Like what other form of employment was he ever going to get into with a name like that? Seriously, what do parents think when they name their children?

We headed to the nearest pirate bar, yes they have bars, and started asking the locals who was Captain Hooks biggest enemy and where could we find them. Turns out that there is a big thing in pirate culture of not telling nose pokey people much at all unless you are dangling from a 30 story building being held up by a robot with razor sharp grabbers... Sara did tell me their technical name, but they look like grabbers, so they are grabbers.

After the first few people ended up being puddles on the ground floor, mainly due to the fact that some pirates actually go for the wooden peg leg thing as a fashion statement... and peg legs tend to not be held on very well, much to my great amusement, we got some solid intel on who Captain Hooks nemesis was. His main nemesis turned out to be his wife, Mrs Hook... again yes that was her actual name... who calls their child Mrs? Then again, what kind of sick and twisted bastard names their child Cedrick Spencer O'Beard...

We headed for her base of operations, a shanty town clinging to a local asteroid belt, and Darren and Sara went about earning their nicknames. I spent the time making sure no-one was hiding in the local tavern, and securing the armoury as well, which just happened to have been located in a house of earthly delights.

When Darren and Sara had finished, there was a body count high enough to earn them a place on the Peacekeepers payroll, and me another promotion for delegation. Then the messy business started with the procurement of the heads of the pirate gang. This me and Darren left to Sara to sort out.

Turns out that when someone asks for the heads of their enemies served up on a silver platter, most people don't actually literally mean that they want the heads of their enemies served up on a silver platter... Captain Hook and his merry band of pirates really were not expecting to see their dinners so shortly after eating them that's for sure. You would think a group of blood thirsty pirates, known for their callous and deadly raids on civilian ships, the murder of a school load of kids, and the burning down of three medical stations would have more stomach for gruesome scenes... apparently not. Either way, we were inducted into their ranks that night and by morning the whole gang was arrested and grateful to be led away from the three psychopaths who had been torturing them... whomever they were.

Once Darren and Sara were given badges, and I got command over my own division, we started chasing after people we wanted to, and taking contracts for whomever we chose... or just making up contracts and trying to come up with reasons why they were wanted. The bosses were always amazed that we had a 100% procurement record for outlaws... Even if some of those outlaws turned out to be royalty. But hey, our job was to catch them, not convict them after all, and as they say, let god sort out the details... or at least the leech lawyers. This was probably the most productive time the Peacekeepers had known, and more people were brought to justice than had ever been in its entire history before we joined. We were able to catch people committing crimes, that even the authorities were unaware of... mainly due to our connections with the criminal underworld... but also because we caught people committing crimes that they didn't even know they were committing.

Considering who we were, corruption also reached an all-time low as well. Strangely that happened after we found out that a corporation had somehow managed to get dirt on one of the presidents that oversaw a section of the Outersphere called the Northern United States Of Awesomeness (Yes, this was their name, and yes they really were that full of themselves). The then president had decided that placing restrictions on information and freedom of expression and movement at the behest of his corporate masters, and while this wouldn't normally be a peacekeeper thing, we got wind of it, and fabricated... I mean discovered through a complex and very long winded (hence the hefty bill we charged the Peacekeepers) investigation. We then assaulted the planet base he had constructed, and arrested him and placed a much more moderate and friendly person in charge until democratic elections could be fabricated... I mean held. We then televised the punishment that was being doled out by Viola and broadcast it to the entire Outersphere, under the title of "*What happens to Corrupt Officials*". This is still one of the most up voted videos of all time... We even have t-shirts on sale in the OZ shop that have the famous last words of "*Please… Not the Peanut Butter!*" printed on the back. It still amazes me how many corrupt individuals handed themselves over and ceased all operations after that video went viral. It also still amazes me that people can look at peanut butter let alone eat it after that too.

Violates also got the 'Best Smile During Something Awful' award, which she keeps above her bed, and managed to secure a contract designing torture devices throughout the Outersphere, and beyond. Some of her designs are being used in some of the most heinous regimes throughout the known universe, a fact that she never lets me forget when I complain about my computer terminal not working as well as it should.

What is the melting point for high carbon titanium alloy? And at what point should sprinklers cease to pump steam into a room full of electrical devices?... ok... I definitely heard a pop on the outer hull that time!... and why is Viola asking Cali to head to the armoury?

Talking of Cali heading to an armoury, that gets me in mind of the time that we decided to invade the Centre home system in order to get some high tech thingamawhatsit that Viola wanted.

Me, unfortunately Derv, Benny and Cali headed off in one of the Cruisers we had requisitioned during one of our many 'Liberation' missions while we worked as a mercenary group. This particular model was a White Petal Corps "*Dragonlilly-Effortlessly-Flies-In-A-Neverending-Celestial-Eververse*" or "*Defiance*" as we had shortened its name to, partly because we couldn't be bothered saying the full name all the time, and partly because it sounded way cooler. We had chosen a White Petal Corps cruiser for several reasons, mainly as it had the longest range scanners out of all of our ships at the time, but also because it had the best sound system. Say what you will about the WPC naming conventions, but they kit their ships with some kick assed audio equipment.

So there we were, flying straight to the Centre's home planet of Tera, music blaring, and desperately trying to ignore the fact that Derv was talking about some wax or other he had come across, when the long range scanners lit up like an arcade that was haunted by a pinball fanatic, and we all quickly jumped to action, and not at all taking the time to shush Derv from talking anymore. It turned out that while the Centre home planet was still there, it was currently under attack coincidentally by the WPC, and for all intense purposes, we were the back up the WPC troops had been waiting for. This would normally have been a stroke of good luck, however, this meant that we were now stuck between a rock and a hard place. Either we helped the WPC out, or reveal the fact that we were currently aboard a stolen cruiser, while conversely having to invade the Centre's most heavily fortified planet defence network on behalf of the WPC, or informing them that no we weren't with the WPC guys, and we just happened across this cruiser, and just happened to appear at the exact same time that the WPC had sent out a request for reinforcements, and could they nicely not try and shoot us out of the system… Either way we were headed for some very hot water. So we did what any self-respecting mercenary does, we flipped a coin. This of course happened to coincide with the gravity system failing aboard the ship, and so the coin landed sideways on, spinning. The only conclusion we could come to was that we were supposed to tell both sides to suck it, and go in all guns blazing… Which I think may have made Cali very happy as she calmly stepped away from the gravity controls and jumped a literal hoop. Benny then started jumping around like an idiot totally unaware of what was actually happening, just because Cali was doing it, and Derv ran his hands through his hair, meanwhile, I made mental calculations about ordinance requirements, the ships current weapons loadouts, where the nearest escape pods were located, and how fast each person in the room could run, and decided it would be better if the others would calm the hell down, and get to work.

What followed next was one of those occasions where we were in the right place at the right time, while normally, flying in all guns blazing would have had at least several of the two sides, that were slogging it out in orbit, turn and blow us out of the sky, the WPC seemed too focused on what they were doing to notice that one of their ships was attacking everything in sight... that or they were just taking too long to tell their commanders what was happening, and so we were getting away with it.

The Order defence ships also seemed none too fussed about the fact that the newly arrived WPC cruiser was shooting everyone and everything in sight since they were too busy trying to deal with the already large numbers of WPC that were there in the first place. We only realised that neither side was particularly bothered with us after we had already shot down one or two of the enemy ships, and decided to stop and try and make a break for the science station orbiting on the other side of the planet… I say we stopped when we realised this, but truth be told, we stopped cause we had run out of ammo since the person in charge of loading the ship with supplies had decided in their infinite wisdom that twenty tonnes of hair care products were more important than twenty tonnes of ammo clips for the ships main cannons. Derv very nearly found his way out of an air lock at this point, but was saved by the fact that we were very much too focused on staying alive rather than pushing him out of said airlock… besides in all the confusion, none of us had remembered to turn the music off, and all Benny heard was *"Push Derv's Hair lock"* which caused Benny to give Derv his comb from in Derv's back pocket… To this day Derv thinks Benny really cares about Derv looking great at all times, and Benny doesn't understand why I don't ask him to do anything more complicated than "Smash", "Kill" and "Carry". Cali at this point noticed that the science station that we were heading towards seemed to be in a panic at the sight of a WPC cruiser heading its way as it had started flashing the inter-galactically accepted signal for "*Please don't shoot us, we surrender*", which was to turn all of its lights into the three colours of Blue, White, and Red, it's the space equivalent of waiving a white flag and putting your arms up in the air… also known as doing a François.

This was a serious stroke of luck for us at this point as we hadn't actually thought about how we were going to get aboard the science station up until this point.

We proceeded to dock at the science station, and tear arse towards their research and development wing, where we found Viola's "*Project X*", which turned out to be a new type of frictionless servo motor that she wanted for her robots. After the initial sighs of "*Well that was underwhelming*", and Cali's "*I was hoping for more explosions to be honest*", we grabbed the super-secret-one-of-a-kind-glorified-hair-dryer motor, and started to head towards the dock again, but thankfully for the interest of this particular story, the Order had sent a couple of Elite Cleaners to try and retake the station, and Cali had the bright idea of checking the Armoury.

Along the way, we ended up fighting a running battle with the Elites that reminded me of a scene from an old game called "*343 - Cortana's Big Day Out*", as we had stealthy fucks dropping out of the woodwork trying to hit us with energy blades, little guys whose heads kept exploding when I shot them, and fired more bullets at one another than should be humanly possible to carry. Thankfully, the science station we were currently on was extremely well armoured inside, and had a very lapse cleaning strategy, as after every corridor we had fought our way down, there were some very handily left piles of ammunition for us to reload our weapons... I even found a resupply cabinet that had my exact ammunition type already loaded into frighteningly similar hand cannons to my own. What added to the comparison between this situation and the aforementioned game was the fact that Cali had somehow managed to get the station to play rousing orchestral pieces through the PA systems that seemed to be going along with the action around us.

The fact that I kept shouting "*Head Shot*" every time I shot one of the bad guys, and Benny would subsequently cheer was eerily similar too... It would be too much if one of us had taken a wrong turn and found a skull just lying on the ground. I guess that's where the similarities ended, as I am pretty sure that if we had died, we wouldn't have respawned at the previous armed checkpoint... Though we did score each other on gruesomeness of kills... Benny kind of won that though, he placed one of the Elites between his butt cheeks and squeezed, while farting in the poor guys face... Poor bastard wished he had been shot by explosive rounds that burn like a sun... he even tried to mumble something along the lines of "*Shoot me in the face, not the chest, not the neck, shoot me in the face, I want to die... now... please god, shoot me in the face*". I have never heard a trained Elite military unit cry with such passion as when they saw their buddies head explode... even me and Cali were kind of glad he finally died, it was truly cruel on Benny's part. The worst thing was how happy Benny seemed after he had done it. He jumped about giggling with the poor guys lifeless corpse dangling behind him like a floppy, bloody, Dingle-berry.

Upon arriving at the armoury, we discovered several projects that may have actually been of more importance than our new hairdryer, even if Derv was totally enamoured by the thing. The first project we came across was an Ammo Generator for small cruiser ships, much like the one we had arrived in, which was good for Derv's long term survival, and the second was a new type of suit that the Order had been co-developing with the Peacekeepers, that would allow someone to stand on the outside of a ship while re-entering an atmosphere…

I think I just worked out why Cali and Viola are headed to the Armoury… I also think I might have worked out why I thought I saw Benny outside the ship waving and smiling at me a moment ago… I thought it might have been the fire suppressant gasses messing with my head again…

Ok, I guess story times over, I must check to see if they are about to do something reckless... and if they aren't, ask them if I could do something reckless, as that would make a great story for my next book... If we survive that is... and if I can manage to not fall down this big gaping hole that just opened up in front of me where the captain's chair used to be... Maybe we should have invested in a brand new ships computer system rather than one of those budget jobs by Dell...

19734388R00038

Printed in Great Britain
by Amazon